The Attempted

Assassination

of

John F. Kennedy

A Political Fantasy

Robert Reginald
(writing as Lucas Webb)

WILDSIDE PRESS

Library of Congress Cataloging in Publication Data

Webb, Lucas, 1948 —
    The attempted assassination of John F. Kennedy.

    1. Kennedy, John Fitzgerald, Pres. U.S., 1917-1963 —
Fiction. I. Title.
PZ4.W36656at   [PS3573.E196]   813'.5'4   76-40282
ISBN 0-89370-204-8

For Richard and Louise,
this small measure
of my affection

MR. PETERSON: We want to thank you, Lord President, for giving us this opportunity to interview you on the eve of your inauguration. This is the Public Eye, a weekly television series spotlighting people in the news today. I'm your host, Miles Peterson, Washington correspondent for the Independent Broadcasting System, and my colleagues for tonight's show are Janet Harrington, columnist for the *Washington Digest*, and Steven Thomas, representing the Federal Cooperative Network of North America. We will begin the questioning with Mr. Thomas.

MR. THOMAS: Thank you, Miles. Lord President, you received an overwhelming popular mandate in the recent elections, some 74% of the votes cast, according to figures released by the National Polling Center. That's the highest percentage accorded a presidential candidate in the last hundred years. How do you think this unprecedented show of support will affect your proposed reorganization plans?

THE PRESIDENT: Well, Steve, you and I both know that the public can change its mind almost as fast as a politician can. I appreciate very much the confidence shown me by the American people, and I'll do everything in my power to maintain it. That doesn't mean, however, that I'll shirk unpopular decisions when they have to be made, or avoid controversial issues just to keep those percentages up. I remember very well how Lord President Kennedy started his administration with a high approval rating, and then watched it steadily drop as the Vietnam War dragged on. Nixon and Freedman also suffered from "pollitis," Nixon because of Watergate, and Freedman over the South African intervention. I think any president has to expect that some of his decisions won't please all the people all of the time, and be willing to live with the consequences. I don't necessarily expect everyone to approve everything I've done or will do; I do ask that they respect my good intentions and my integrity. I'll do the best I can for all Americans.

MR. THOMAS: To return to your proposals, sir; what do you think are your chances of getting them through Congress?

THE PRESIDENT: *(pauses)* Steve, these ideas of mine aren't particularly new or revolutionary, and I certainly haven't made any secret of them during my campaign.

Presumably, those who voted for me were aware of my recommendations, and either approved of them, or at least didn't sufficiently disapprove to vote for my opponent. Now, I have to regard that kind of mandate as significant, and I think the House and Senate would be foolish to ignore the will of the people. We've just begun a new century, and we're long overdue for a few changes in the way we do our everyday business. The people have made it quite clear time and again during the last twenty-six years, ever since the Watergate Affair, that they want an honest, efficient government, and by God, I intend to make it so. Ms. Harrington.

MS. HARRINGTON: Thank you, Lord President. All of Washington has been talking about the Vice President-elect, the first black woman to be chosen for that office. How do you envision her role in the new government?

THE PRESIDENT: Lady Jordan is amply qualified in every respect to assume the Lord Presidency, if that should be necessary, having had executive and legislative experience as a Congressperson, Senator, and ˜Supreme Governor of the State of Texas. I wouldn't have chosen her if I'd felt otherwise. The problem I'm facing today is the problem faced by every lord president of the last fifty years: now that I've got this multi-talented person on my staff, how do I best utilize her many endowments? Part of this challenge is answered by my reorganization plan, which specifies in greater detail the role of the Vice President, and expands his or her role to include additional duties in the legislative branch, or, at the option of the executive, appointment to a cabinet-level position, with actual administrative duties. This should help make her an integral part of my administration from the very beginning. Yes, Mr. Peterson.

MR. PETERSON: Sir, you'll be sworn in tomorrow as the 42nd Lord President of the United States. What do you intend to tell the American people in your inaugural address?

THE PRESIDENT: Well, Mr. Peterson, if I told you that, I wouldn't have much of anything to say tomorrow. And while that might make some of my opponents (and friends) happy, I'd prefer to wait until the occasion itself before starting my soliloquy. I will say this, however: I think we need to restore America's faith in itself before we can restore its faith in government. My administration will be an honest one, and as efficient as men can make it.

MR THOMAS: Lord President, we've talked in general terms about what you intend to do once you're sworn in; I wonder if we could begin discussing specifics.

THE PRESIDENT: Please go ahead, Steve.

MR. THOMAS: Let's start first with foreign affairs. Relations with the United States of Europe have become strained in the last few years, beginning with the Rouen incident. How do you intend to improve our ties with the European nation?

THE PRESIDENT: I have already made a tentative agreement to visit the USE in May of this year, beginning with a reception in Paris on the 16th. King Henri of France will serve as host, and I understand the Lord Chancellor and Premier have expressed great interest in the prospect of meeting me the next day. My itinerary also includes a stopover in London, on May 20th, which will commence with a visit to King Charles; I'll meet with Prime Minister Thorp of England that evening, and with Prime Minister MacDonald of Scotland on the 21st. During the next week, I'll be touring Belgium, The Netherlands, Denmark, and Norway. The trip will end in West Germany, where I'm scheduled to confer with Kaiser Ludwig and Mr. Muller on the 28th. I'm hoping these personal contacts between governmental officials will lead to a new era of understanding between America and the USE. Incidentally, I've been invited to address the European Parliament in Brussels on May 30th. Ms. Harrington.

MS. HARRINGTON: What do you think about the Indian situation?

THE PRESIDENT: Well, Janet, I'm not really sure there's anything anyone can do at this point. We have a situation here where the government has disintegrated into chaos, the people are starving, and China is threatening to move in. The basic problem is one that the Government of India has overlooked all these years, and that's the population explosion. India has persistently refused to accept reality, and adopt measures to control the productiveness of its own people. The direct consequence of its irresponsibility is mass famine, and a gradual decline into barbarism. I don't like to watch the news reports any more than you do, but I also don't like the idea of interfering in another county's internal affairs. The United States no longer has the kinds of food surpluses it had back in the '60s and '70s, and I'm not willing to destroy what little reserves we have just to bolster the Indian government, and that's all we'd be doing by sending them grain. As far as I can see, the situation is irretrievable: a great many people are going to die, and there's absolutely nothing we can do about it.

MR. PETERSON: Sir, we've heard a great deal about your career in the last few months, but none of the many reports on your life have really identified the beginning of your interest in politics. Where did it start?

THE PRESIDENT: You know, Miles, I'm not really too sure I can answer that one. When did you decide to become a reporter? These things are rarely clear cut, even in one's own mind. They tend to evolve over a period of years, as one gradually comes to the realization of what he or she wants to do. For me, I guess, my first moment of political awareness, if you want to call it that, was that dismal November afternoon thirty-seven years ago when John Kennedy was shot in Dallas. I was just sixteen at the time, attending high school in Spokane, Washington, and I remember very clearly the announcement coming over the loud-speaker. Shots had been fired at the Kennedy entourage, but nobody really knew what was going on. And then we heard that Kennedy himself had been wounded. It occurred to me suddenly how important one man could be, and how much difference it would make to the world if Kennedy died. There aren't very many men whose life or death could change history, but Kennedy was one of them, and I was determined to join that exclusive group if I could. The rest you know.

MS. HARRINGTON: Then your goal from the beginning of your career was the lord presidency?

THE PRESIDENT: (laughs) I suppose that's the El Dorado of any politician. You start thinking of what you could do if you were sitting in that chair, and you know you'll never be satisfied with anything less. Of course, you also realize that 99% of the lot never get that far, that the odds are clearly stacked against you, and so you steel yourself against

the ultimate disappointment. I find myself wondering sometimes how I ever managed to get here. It's like a dream to
me — but a very pleasant one. Yes, Steve.

MR. THOMAS: During your campaign,
you promised to pardon any draft evaders still at large from
the South African troubles. Do you still intend to keep that
pledge, after hearing the protests last week of the South
African refugees in Arizona?

THE PRESIDENT: It seems to me that the
only way we can put the South African War behind us is by
pardoning all the young men who fled the country or went
underground to avoid doing what they felt was wrong. I don't
deny that some of them were shirkers, and others may well
have been morally weak, or wrong in their judgments. I do say
that it's time to lay such considerations aside, and forgive
those who declined to participate in the American intervention overseas. To that end, I will formally issue a presidential
proclamation upon assuming office tomorrow, and forever end
the mass outlawing of a large portion of our younger generation.

MR. PETERSON: Lord President, as part of
my preparation for this interview, I've been reading all three
of your published books relating to American politics, and
I've been struck by your forceful analyses of recent history,
and, in particular, your evident admiration of Lord President
John IV Kennedy, a figure who has not been well-favored by
most historians of modern times. Why your devotion to this
particular man?

THE PRESIDENT: Well, Miles, I think he's
been badly maligned, to be quite frank. Take the Cuban
incident, for example. Kennedy inherited a plan from
Eisenhower that was based upon wrong information, and
wrong suppositions, and was forced to act very quickly after
assuming office, under great pressure from the military and
the CIA. He made the wrong decision, obviously. We should
not have attempted to invade Cuba, which had and has a right
to its own government, chosen by any means it sees fit. But
Kennedy, unlike many leaders before and since, had the
ability to admit his mistakes when he made them, and learn
from his misjudgments, thereby growing in his office. I like
that kind of man.

MR. PETERSON: But surely, he made the same mistake again when he involved us in the Vietnam conflict. Or would you disagree?

THE PRESIDENT: I would. Kennedy made the best decision he could with the information he had available. You must remember that even lord presidents aren't omniscient. They rely heavily upon their staffs, and the federal bureaucracy in general. In Kennedy's case, he derived his day-to-day information on the military situation in southeast Asia from the Lord Chief-of-Staff of the Armed Forces, his cabinet officers, and his personal counselors, all of whom tended to view things in a particular way. And Kennedy himself was a man of action; he preferred to do something, and perhaps be forced to live with the consequences, than to do nothing. At the same time, he was an inexperienced administrator, having had few executive opportunities in the Senate, and was perhaps a bit naive. Everyone in government tends to regard his own position as important, usually more important than everyone else's, and everyone naturally tries to increase his or her importance in any way possible. The name of the game is power; the rules vary from person to person, but tend to be nonexistent near the top. Truth, what there is of it, is altered to suit the situation. Efficiency is less important than self-aggrandizement, job performance is judged primarily in terms of personal loyalty to one's administrators, and promotions nearly always result from expert boot-licking on the right occasions. No one sticks his neck out for any reason other than self-advancement. That's the way our government really operates, and it is, I admit, a cynical way of looking at things. Administrations may change, but the bureaucracy forever stays the same. It's very difficult to break through the circle of one's advisers, even under the best of circumstances. Since they've all been appointed by the administrator, they all tend to tell him or her exactly what he or she wants to hear. Simultaneously, they can easily become censors when the flow of information to the administrator becomes so vast that it must necessarily be reduced to a bearable level; usually, that reduction is handled by the lord president's staff: what he ultimately gets affects the way he thinks. I once read a story where a man set out to attain final power in his world. He progressively rose through the administrative ranks of his government, until he finally got himself elected to the supreme council, and was eventually chosen its chair. Then he discovered, much to his surprise, that the council based its decisions on information fed to it by a bank of computers, and only rarely deviated from the course indicated on the printouts. He traced the flow of information back down to a lowly clerical employee, who provided all the raw data from which the computer derived its formulations. The poor clerk was suddenly retired, and our hero was hired in his place, where he was finally in a position to affect the course of history. He lived happily ever after. There's a moral in that story for all of us. Kennedy escalated our involvement in Vietnam because he saw no other way out, based upon the data provided him. Once the US was committed to a massive intrusion, a certain amount of self-justification set in at all levels of government, with a lot of wishful thinking. It's very easy to tell oneself, just a little more, just a little longer, and we'll all be out of the woods. Unfortunately for everyone, it didn't happen that way. Eventually, one of the participants had to bow out, and inevitably it had to be us, because the Vietnamese were not just fighting for political or philosophical ends, but for their homeland. As soon as you involve patriotism and nationalism in a war on one side, where the other side has nothing but political interests at stake, you immediately give the first combatant an advantage, irrespective of war material. It took us thousands of lives to realize that, and ultimately, it was the pragmatist, Richard Nixon, who brought the troops home, not because he particularly wanted to, but because he had to if he ever wanted to get reelected. And one somehow got the feeling that reelection was a large part of it. Mr. Thomas.

MR. THOMAS: You obviously have a rather low opinion of Lord President Nixon. Exactly how does he differ, in your estimation, from Kennedy, Carter, or some of the more recent lord presidents, like Sanders and Rogers?

THE PRESIDENT: It seems to me, Steve, that a man is measured by the kinds of things he does in life. Everyone receives a certain share of opportunities, and luck, of course, plays its role in this; but luck has only a limited part in life, and a person has only himself to blame if he blows his chances. Nixon's a good example of how a person can go wrong in little ways. From the beginning of his term, he knew that he had the confidence of less than half the people, having been elected with just 43% of the vote. The Democrats controlled Congress, and although the Republicans made strenuous efforts throughout Nixon's term to gain a majority in the

12.

Senate, they didn't even come close (in fact, they never seated a majority in either house again). Combine these realities with the crises the US was experiencing overseas, the riots and demonstrations at home, and we have a situation that was very difficult indeed. All of these danger signals should have been sufficient warning to keep a low profile and walk very softly and carefully around each problem area. The country needed a soother, not a shouter, and Nixon failed to meet this challenge. By using a heavy hand wherever possible, he alienated millions of Americans. The way he employed Vice President Agnew reflected credit on neither of them, and he surrounded himself with self-seeking advisers who virtually manipulated the executive by restricting the flow of visitors and information. A crisis was inevitable.

MR. THOMAS: Of course, Nixon claimed to his dying day that he had no advance knowledge of the Watergate break-in, that he never condoned lawlessness among his staff, that the press manipulated the public into believing that he was guilty of crimes he never committed, or even knew about until after they were exposed.

THE PRESIDENT: Still, he set the tone for his administration. Look, Steve, if I hired you to guard my store, if I had a store, and I came in one day to find that half the place was gone, I'd be justifiably angry, wouldn't I? Here I'd been paying you to watch over my goods, to protect my livelihood, and you had either been so lax as not to notice someone stealing them, or had fallen asleep on the job, or, even worse, had been bribed to let someone take them. I've not only lost my investment, but also the money I'd been putting into your salary. I'd have been better off if I'd simply bought myself a better lock. I feel the same way about Nixon. In the end, the worth of the man was revealed by the actions he took to ensure his reelection. Whether he knew the specific details really isn't as relevant as he seemed to think. I've never been particularly concerned about that part of it. What has always bothered me is the environment he created, in which semilegal or even illegal acts were condoned or justified as part of the working atmosphere of his administration. His main rationale for all this seemed to be his own continuance in office, the kind of egoism that says a particular person is necessary to the state. Towards the end of his term, everything else was sublimated to that one goal; increasingly, the many problems that required his attention were put aside, as he spent more and more time fighting the slow, inexorable forces that were engulfing him. A sad case in every way. What made it even sadder was the man's obvious intelligence; Richard Nixon singlehandedly did more for American foreign policy than any lord president in the preceding twenty years. Some of the impetus came from Baron Kissinger, of course, but he had to have the president's backing and confidence to make even the slightest move towards the Chinese People's Empire, to cite just one example.

MS. HARRINGTON: I wonder if I could return to more immediate concerns, Lord President.

THE PRESIDENT: Yes, of course, Janet. Excuse me for rambling on; I enjoy talking, and it's very easy to get carried away.

MS. HARRINGTON: Sir, the right-to-life groups have been lobbying recently for a constitutional amendment to end voluntary euthanasia. Where do you stand on this issue?

THE PRESIDENT: I'm against it, as I would be against any amendment that's legally unnecessary.

MS. HARRINGTON: But in this case, sir, the Supreme Court has thrown out all laws restricting voluntary euthanasia. Wouldn't it take a constitutional amendment to restore the ban?

THE PRESIDENT: That's true, Janet, but I am unalterably opposed to amendments that restrict the individual's right to do what he pleases with his own body. We had a similar situation twenty or thirty years ago, when another group of misguided individuals attempted to amend the Constitution to prohibit abortions. Personally, I find abortions repugnant, from just about every possible viewpoint; if you're going to practice birth control, the time to do it is before you go to bed, not afterwards. But if someone wants to have an abortion, I don't think we ought to interfere. I'm not saying, mind, that everyone *must* have an abortion, and I'm not even saying that every doctor must participate; what I am saying is that it should be a matter of personal choice. Those who find it morally reprehensible need not participate, and if they can convince the rest of humanity that their views are right and just, so be it. But let's not write such convictions into the Constitution. As it happened, the abortion groups were never able to convince a majority of the American people that their position was right, and the proposed amendments failed. I hope and trust the same thing will happen today.

MS. HARRINGTON: The euthanasia groups say they're only attempting to outlaw legal murder.

THE PRESIDENT: Is it moral, then, to make unreasonable efforts to sustain life even when there's no possibility that the person involved will ever be able to function as a human being again? That kind of argument angers me. We now have machines that will continue bodily functions indefinitely; scientists have told me that theoretically they can now keep us going for fifty or a hundred years beyond the normal life span of Homo sapiens. But is it right to do so? You see, the one problem with this entire business is that we haven't yet found any way of slowing down or arresting the decay of the mind, the one thing that distinguishes men from brute animals. They can replace all the parts except that one, and that's the only one that really matters. I'd rather not live than live to be a 150-year-old vegetable. If I can't enjoy life, why bother? Mr. Peterson, you've been rather quiet for the past few moments.

MR. PETERSON: Not intentionally, sir, let me assure you. An item on the service wires last week indicated that Nigeria had become the 45th nation to explode an atom bomb. What do you think can be done to halt the proliferation of nuclear weapons?

THE PRESIDENT: At this point, nothing. Too many countries have them, and too many others could have them if they wanted them. A college student could make one, if he had the raw materials. The time for reasonable efforts at control has long since passed. I would welcome more signatures on the various test ban treaties that have been put forward in the last thirty years, but practically, I see no way of enforcing them short of war, and that's precisely what the treaties are supposed to prevent.

MR. THOMAS: People's Tsar Sergei Tigranovich Machmudov said in a speech New Year's Day that he would welcome better Soviet-American relations. What are your feelings on this subject?

THE PRESIDENT: Pretty much the feelings of all Americans, I think: we would all welcome better relations with all our earthly neighbors. The question is, do the Soviets really want better relations, or are they just saying so to gain a short term advantage in a long term struggle? Judging from past experiences, I think I'd be very hesitant to accept too much of what the Soviets say on face value, although I welcome the People's Tsar's speech, and I hope that we can meet personally shortly after I take office. Ms. Harrington.

MS. HARRINGTON: You're the first lord president ever elected from the Pacific Northwest. How does that make you feel?

THE PRESIDENT: Gratified. *(laughter)* Mr. Peterson.

MR. PETERSON: When will you be moving into the White House, sir?

THE PRESIDENT: Sometime next week, my wife tells me; she's handling all the details.

MR. PETERSON: Why is that, Lord President?

THE PRESIDENT: Well, she told me some time ago that she didn't want me to have anything to do with it, and I decided it was better to follow her advice in this matter. *(laughter)*

MR. PETERSON: I understand, sir.

THE PRESIDENT: Mary has been in contact this past week with the Lord President's wife, Lady Louise Rogers, and she tells me that everything is coming along very smoothly, and we should start settling in next Monday. Lord Rogers will apparently retire to his estate near Paradise Valley, California, though you'd have to get confirmation of his plans directly from him, I think. He's been very gracious in offering assistance to all members of the new administration, and I want to thank him publicly for his help in getting through the bureaucratic tape. It's made life much easier for everyone. I also want to accept his kind offer to act as a general counselor to the Lord President during the transitional months of my administration; his advice will prove to be a great asset, I'm sure.

MS. HARRINGTON: I think our viewers would be interested in knowing what you do to relax, in your leisure time?

THE PRESIDENT: It's been so long since I had any leisure time to worry about that I'm not sure I can remember. I read a lot, primarily science fiction novels, when I have the chance. I also enjoy walking, particularly in semi-mountainous regions, and some recreational sports, like badminton, ping pong, light games. And I write a little when I'm in the mood.

MS. HARRINGTON: I've read all of your books. Have you done anything besides political studies?

THE PRESIDENT: In my younger days, I wrote some fiction and verse. But I don't do much anymore; it requires more time and concentration than I can afford to give it, and I'd rather not do anything unless I can do it right.

MS. HARRINGTON: You wrote poetry? Could you give us an example of your work?

THE PRESIDENT: Well, I could try, if you really want to hear something. *(mummers of approval)* Very well, then; this is one of my favorites. It has no title:

Your heart is open to mine eyes, as clear
Before me as your face recumbent on
My shoulder. I can feel your warmth, and hear
The sigh of your breath. There's a smile upon
Your lips. But still the demons trouble me,
And bid me look again. "Those lines," they say,
"Those crooked scars of time; when will they flee
Away?" And yet I love you. When I weigh
The cumbrances of age against the love
You give so freely, how can I resist?
You've renewed my spirit, partaken of
My life, and made of me your loyalist.
    Then why these doubts that nothing can dispel?
    I know your heart too little — or too well!

ALL: Thank you, Lord President.

MR. THOMAS: Sir, if we could get back
to business . . .

THE PRESIDENT: Of course, Mr. Thomas.

MR. THOMAS: Well, sir, the National
Party still controls the House of Representatives, and I was
wondering if you anticipate any difficulties working with the
leadership there.

THE PRESIDENT: Steve, I'm always willing
to meet with the leaders of the House, on any occasion where
it might be of use. And I don't think I'll prove inflexible,
either on legislative matters, or anything else. On the other
hand, I am making some serious and well-considered proposals
for governmental reorganization, and I expect them to receive
the attention they deserve. I will be most happy to work with
any members of the House or Senate to get these proposals
passed intact.

MR. PETERSON: Different lord presidents
have handled their relationships with the press in different
ways. What will Lord President Lister do?

THE PRESIDENT: Well, I hope he'll do a
little better job than some of his predecessors. *(laughter)*
Seriously, Miles, I think that good relations with the press are
exceptionally important to any public figure — that's why
I'm meeting with you here tonight — and I intend to do the
best I can to make them cordial and easy-going at all times. I
hope to hold regular press conferences every Monday morning
at ten o'clock, except when I'm out of town on business or
vacation. One reporter from every major news agency will be
given permanent status, and the rest will be rotated by lot.
Questions will be allowed on all subjects, although I don't
necessarily guarantee an answer to everyone of them. If I
don't like the questions, believe me, I'll tell you so.

MR. THOMAS: I'm sure you will, sir.
Imperial Leader Wang Min-t'ang of the Chinese People's
Empire is visiting the Kingdom of Hawaii this week, seeking
to renew the ties established five years ago between Honolulu
and Peking. King Kalakaua II has reassured the Chinese leader
of the eternal friendship between their two nations, and has
pledged his assistance in overthrowing the imperialistic aims of
the United States. What is your reaction to his statement?

18.

THE PRESIDENT: China and Hawaii are perfectly free, in my opinion, to do as they please, so long as they don't immediately threaten the security of the United States. Talk is just that, and as long as it remains that I foresee no difficulties in our relationships with either of those countries. Certainly Hawaii has every reason to be wary of the American state, since a group of American merchants tried to overthrow the monarchy there in 1893. Fortunately, Lord President Cleveland intervened, and restored Queen Liliuokalani to her throne later that same year. Every other attempt to annex the islands to this country has been defeated, and rightfully so. The United States has no claims or designs upon the Kingdom of Hawaii, and hopes to continue its cordial relations with that country indefinitely.

MS. HARRINGTON: Do you have any comments to make upon the outgoing administration of Lord President Richard II Rogers?

THE PRESIDENT: Not really, Janet; I think it would be inappropriate for me to comment upon the man I'm replacing. History will render its judgment in due course, but I think it would be somewhat precipitous on my part to begin compiling that record now. I will say that I've had very good relations with the Lord President since being elected, and I respect his opinions very highly. They've been based, after all, on a great deal of practical experience, the kind only eight years in office can bring.

MR. THOMAS: Do you intend to run for reelection four years hence?

THE PRESIDENT: Provided that my health remains good, yes.

MR. PETERSON: I'd like to return for a moment to Lord President Kennedy, if I might.

THE PRESIDENT: Certainly, Miles.

MR. PETERSON: There are some who say the CIA was involved in the shooting at Dallas in 1963, and that a massive conspiracy was responsible for planning the entire incident. Certainly, the killing of Lee Harvey Oswald so soon after he was arrested seems suspicious. Do you have any comments to make about the Kennedy shooting?

THE PRESIDENT: I don't really think this particular theory has been proved or disproved, and quite frankly, I doubt that it will ever be. If indeed there was a conspiracy, those involved in its workings were certainly clever enough to dispose of the evidence a long time ago, and it's extremely unlikely that anything further will surface now. The fact that nothing has ever been conclusively associated with the conspiracy idea seems, in my mind, to lessen its validity. Public figures are really very easy types to kill, because they all follow regular schedules, with lots of publicity; and by killing one of them, a person immediately gains a certain notoriety. Just as the presidency itself is the most sought-after position in the country, so too is the killing of a president the height of infamy. There's a certain warped logic that says, if you're going to do it, you might as well go to the top. For certain types of people, those misfits who've never been able to find their niche in life, such notoriety is the most they can hope for. What I'm saying is that it's quite conceivable that one man could have shot Kennedy; it's much less likely that more than one did, since every additional person involved in a plot is one more who could spill the beans. As far as the CIA is concerned, or any other governmental agency, there's never been any evidence to suggest that they plotted the death of their Commander-in-Chief. Yes, Steve.

MR. THOMAS: Isn't it true, though, that many of the persons who witnessed the shooting died shortly thereafter?

THE PRESIDENT: Some did, some didn't; some are even alive today. It's like the curse of Tutankhamen's tomb, back in the 1920s.: a pharaoh's final resting place is discovered and uncovered, and immediately a number of persons involved in the hunt start falling over. Was there a curse? Or was it just the fancies of idle minds trying to find logical explanations for things which require none? You tell me. People make mistakes, and if there had been a conspiracy behind Kennedy's shooting, certainly it would have come out over the years. Yet it never has.

MS. HARRINGTON: Lord President. to change the subject once again, your daughter has been reported living with a man in Seattle. How do you feel about such relationships?

THE PRESIDENT: When I was growing up, I had a number of friends who shacked up with their girlfriends, so it doesn't really shock me in the least, if that's what you're asking. My daughter's a grown woman, and she's free to do what she likes with her life! I'd be the last person in the world to try and tell her what to do — and she'd be the last to listen, I think. I neither approve nor disapprove. If she loves the young man, that's good enough for me, and I'll respect her choice. Whether or not she goes through the marriage ceremony seems somewhat irrelevant to me, since the measure of one's affection for another person lies not in such mundane things as rings, flowers, or vows, but inside the heart; and all the weddings in the world won't increase one's feelings one iota unless that person already cares. I've known many married couples whose lives were one long hell; conversely, I've known unmarried pairs who were radiantly happy. I think you ought to leave people alone to live their lives as they see fit, and interfere with them as little as humanly possible.

MR. PETERSON: You've said on many occasions that one of your first acts in office will be to seek tax reform. What do you think is wrong with the present system?

THE PRESIDENT: Just about everything, Miles. The whole tax structure is basically unfair, because it places a greater burden on those least able to pay. In theory, it's supposed to work the other way around, but over the years so many loopholes have been added by special interest groups and rich lawyers that the result is so much Swiss cheese: it's full of holes. I want a reasonable tax structure, with no exceptions, no outs for anyone, no misunderstandings of what anyone owes. I don't even particularly care precisely how it's set up, or what the rates are, so long as they're uniformly and fairly applied. Just because Jack Smith's a dogcatcher doesn't mean that he should receive a special exemption for flea powder, which is necessary to his job. That's a ridiculous example, of course, and purposely so, but there are just as many that have actually been put into law.

MR. THOMAS: Although the facts have been published many times, I wonder if you could tell us in your own words something about your career in public office.

THE PRESIDENT: Well, Steve, I graduated from Gonzaga University in 1968, was drafted by the Army and served two years, one in Vietnam. That was 1969, as I recall. Fortunately, I came through without much damage to limb or mind, although I saw some pretty gruesome things over there. War is not a gentle business, and both sides had flashes of excessive brutality.

MR. THOMAS: Did you actually partici-pate in any of the fighting?

THE PRESIDENT: Yes and no. I was trained as a medic, and I was stationed for the most part in base areas. There were several occasions, however, when I was involved in skirmishes, and at least one time, I remember picking up a gun to defend myself. But everything happens so fast in battle that it's difficult afterwards to remember the exact sequence of events. I was lucky; some of my friends weren't so lucky.

MR. THOMAS: When did you actually get involved in politics?

THE PRESIDENT: Actually, I was heavily in-volved while still attending college. Neither Gonzaga nor Spokane could have been regarded as hotbeds of political fervor, at least not when compared to the rest of the nation at that time; the Jebbies, as we called the Jesuit fathers, tended to keep things pretty well under control. I ran for school office several times, even got elected as Vice-President of the Senior Class, and then became involved with Robert Kennedy's bid for the Democratic nomination.

MR. THOMAS: What exactly did you do?

THE PRESIDENT: Very little, when I think of it. *(laughter)* We did all the usual things you do in a cam-paign that both annoy and interest people: we made the rounds of neighborhoods, toting our literature, phoned endless numbers of registered Democrats, and generally made nui-sances of ourselves. I still wonder to this day if Kennedy would have gotten the nomination had he lived. But of course, he was shot in Los Angeles early in June, about the same time I graduated, and the shock of his death, combined with my induction notice, effectively removed me from the scene.

MR. THOMAS: Then you went off to war. When did you return to politics?

THE PRESIDENT: In a way, I don't suppose
I ever left it. Even though I was out of the country for two
years, first in West Germany, and then in Vietnam, I was well
aware of what was happening here. I heard how Johnson, for
example, managed to secure the nomination after Robert
Kennedy's death, and the close election results in the fall,
when Richard Nixon just beat him out by a hair. The difference, I suppose, was that I heard it all at a distance, once-
removed, rather than close at hand, as a participant. But I
tried to keep informed. And my political education pro-
ceeded dramatically on another front, one that I'd never really
experienced before, with my induction into gut politics,
played in the dirtiest way possible. You have to realize, Steve,
that the Army is one of the most convoluted bureaucracies
ever invented by man, and the oil of all bureaucracies is
political favors; it's a lesser form of the pay-off systems you
see so rampant in the Middle East, and in socialized bureaucracies, like the Soviet Union. Instead of cash changing hands,
an intricate system of political IOU's and debits is used to buy
services one might normally expect to receive. In that sense, I
suppose, we're somewhat more sophisticated than the Arabs;
we use checks instead of money rolls. Well, I can recall being
stationed at a base in West Germany, where a flea-bitten old
sergeant had somehow managed to get control of base leaves,
and doled them out one by one to anyone who could pay the
price. The price varied from man to man, depending on each
person's position, rank, and political wealth. He had the best-
stocked larder in town, because everytime one of the cooks
wanted to go off base, cakes, meats, and other special treats
would somehow find their way into this guy's horde. And he
was completely amoral about the whole thing; you either paid
whatever price he wanted, or you just didn't go anywhere. He
could care less whether or not you had a legitimate reason for
taking off, or whether you had actually earned your leave. No
tickee, no washee. He was probably the most hated man on
base, the CO included, but no one was ever able to break the
stranglehold he held on that one key position. In the end, he
was transferred out, but before leaving, he actually sold off
his office to the highest bidder, and then made sure that his
designated heir really succeeded him. This experience taught
me two things: evil people do exist; an honest politician
accepts no gifts. It occurred to me at the time that this mer-
cenary sergeant, although immensely powerful, hadn't the
faintest idea of what to do with his power except feather his
own nest. What a waste of talent! Here was a man who could

have added a great deal to the Army, and instead he used his abilities to prey on a bunch of poor slobs who had almost nothing to begin with. He was a parasite in uniform. You may wonder why the CO didn't clamp down on this guy, and throw him out on his ass. Well, I found out afterwards from a friend that the general in charge of the base used this sergeant to help keep in line a few men who didn't like to play the game the way the general wanted it played. Anyone who didn't applaud loudly enough when the general stepped out of the shower found himself given the runaround anytime he wanted to do something that required formal permission from higher authority.

MR. THOMAS: But surely, Lord President, yours was a unique experience.

THE PRESIDENT: I wish I could say so, Steve, but this kind of creeping corruption seems to permeate every government bureaucracy I've ever been associated with. It's a moral disease, utterly insidious in its effects, spreading slowly but inexorably from person to person in the hier- archical structures of bureaucratic systems. Those who manage to throw off the infection are inevitably scarred by it, and just enough succumb to keep it moving. Let's consider, for a moment, a hypothetical situation. A certain Mr. Thomas is hired into a low-level administrative job by a public agency. This Mr. Thomas happens to be rather more astute than the average Joe, and within a few months he figures out how the game is played, and is immediately faced with a dilemma: does he go along with it, or does he refuse? Because, you see, he discovers that his boss is the kind of guy who doesn't par- ticularly bother with such things as ethics, morals, or doing a good job; those kinds of concerns aren't related to political survival, at least in the eyes of his boss, and so they don't matter very much when matched against such "virtues" as personal loyalty, kowtowing, and bootlicking. There are a number of senior executives in this agency who have rather obviously sold out, since they wouldn't have gotten where they are otherwise; they're mediocre workers, and seem to know relatively little about the jobs they're supposed to be supervising, but they all have one outstanding quality in com- mon: they're intensely loyal to the man who put them there, and they'll do anything whatever that's asked of them. Now, as I said, our Mr. Thomas is somewhat more discerning than most, and he notices a curious thing, what I'll call the King

Henry effect. King Henry VIII, as you perhaps recall, ruled England in the sixteenth century; he was the one with the six wives. In those days, monarchs were absolute rulers of their states; they could do just about anything they pleased, and there was no one to say nay. That wasn't enough for Henry; he also wanted his subjects' willing and wholehearted approval, and not giving one's approval was in itself grounds for treason. Sir Thomas More kept silent about the King's marriage; Henry wanted his acquiescence, as signified by the loyalty oath imposed upon all state officials, and when More declined to swear, he was brought to trial on drummed-up charges sworn with false evidence, and executed. Mr. Thomas's administrator is this kind of man, who not only wants to have his way, but also the applause of his employees. And Mr. Thomas refuses to applaud, although he does his job in every detail to the best of his ability, performs any tasks directly assigned to him, and is, in every other respect, a model employee. The result: Mr. Thomas, although he's retained in his position, will never advance beyond his present low level, despite good and loyal service to the state. He chooses to do that rather than compromise his principles. And yet he is injured to some degree, because all persons want the approval of their fellow beings, and he feels, with some justification, that his talents have been ignored, his good service denigrated, his abilities slighted. His morale declines, his performance levels drop, and he starts looking for a way out, either another job, or a transfer to an equivalent position elsewhere in the system. Thus, the good employee is penalized for his good qualities, and the political hack tends to advance to the top, and there seems no way to change the situation without somehow dismantling the bureaucratic structure that furthers the system. I seem to have gotten a little off the subject, Steve; perhaps you can direct me back to my topic.

MR. THOMAS: We were talking about your career, sir. What did you do after the war?

THE PRESIDENT: I was sent to Vietnam about the time that Nixon was sworn in as Lord President, and spent almost a year there, being released just prior to Chrismas of 1969. When I returned, I enrolled in law school at USC, and three years later passed the bar exam. At about this time, the Watergate mess was coming out, and once more I found myself absorbed in the passage of current history.

MR. THOMAS: You've already indicated your disapproval of Lord President Richard I Nixon; where do you think he went wrong?

THE PRESIDENT: He wasn't honest, either with himself or the American people, and his half-truths and untruths finally caught up with him. Also, he failed to see that the taping system he installed in the White House might prove detrimental to him in the long run, since it recorded everything he said indiscriminately; and in that he failed to see his own character as it really was. He was secretive, and not open, and this hurt him badly, more, I think, than he ever saw himself. He could have overcome his weaknesses had he only realized them, and played against them; but he never did. And the judgment of history has been that he deserved to be impeached and removed from office. I was a lawyer for the district attorney's office in Riverside, California in the summer of 1974, when all of this was coming to a head. I was saddened but relieved when he finally resigned. In the end, one must say that he did the best thing of his political career, and got out when the system required it, with dignity and grace.

MR. THOMAS: And then Lord President Albert succeeded.

THE PRESIDENT: Yes, and it's a curious thing to wonder what might have happened if Congress had adopted a constitutional amendment proposed back in the mid-1960s to regulate presidential succession. There was some concern after the Kennedy shootings that at some point in the future the unthinkable might happen, and both executive offices, Lord President and Vice President, might become vacant simultaneously, thereby creating a governmental crisis. The Speaker of the House, so their thinking went, might well be of the opposite party, and his succession to the office without an actual election would create a vast outcry from those being deprived of power. The resulting chaos would greatly hamper any attempt at administration. Two possible solutions were proposed: an immediate election whenever the lord presidency became vacant, or the appointment of new vice-presidents when required, with the advice and consent of the Congress. Both were discarded, however, for what must be regarded as well-reasoned objections, and nothing was ever done. Consequently, when Agnew resigned in disgrace in 1973, and Nixon followed suit the next year, the Speaker of the House became Lord President.

MR. THOMAS: How do you assess his
administration?

THE PRESIDENT: He was the right man for
the right time. After the chaos and uproar of the Nixon years,
we needed a man who was calm, quiet, and down-to-earth, and
Albert was that man. As I recall, one of his first public state-
ments specifically disavowed any attempt on his part to run
again. He had originally intended to retire in 1977, he said,
and his succession to the lord presidency had in no way
changed his plans. He also said that he had never really wanted
the job, but he'd do the best he could, since he hadn't any
choice in the matter. Albert was a wise man, in the sense of
understanding his own limitations, and while he didn't accomplish many tangible goals during his administration, he did
restore the balance between the executive and legislative
branches of government, and that was no small feat. His wide
experience in the House helped him create smooth channels of
communication between the White House and Capitol Hill;
one got the impression that government in general was back on
the right track. The only controversy that sprang up during his
three years in office was the pardoning of Richard Nixon.
Legal authorities remain divided to this day on the question of
whether or not he did the right thing, but once accomplished,
of course, a pardon can never be revoked, so perhaps it's after
the fact. Nixon, as you may recall, escaped impeachment by
resigning, but he was still legally liable for his actions. He and
his colleagues were brought to trial during the ensuing months,
and were all found guilty of various charges associated with
the Watergate break-in and its coverup. Just before Nixon was
to be sentenced, Albert released a statement saying that the
poor man had suffered enough, and would continue to suffer,
now that the public record had established his guilt before a
jury of his peers beyond any reasonable doubt. Since the Constitution forbad cruel and unusual punishment, Albert had
therefore pardoned the former Lord President, and he was free
to return to his western retreat. Which, of course, he did, until
his death in 1984.

MR. THOMAS: It was about this time, I
believe, that you were getting involved in politics yourself.

THE PRESIDENT: Yes, Steve; in November,
1975, I'd heard Jimmy Carter speak before a group of
attorneys, and I decided then that he had the best chance of

getting the Democratic nomination, despite the large number of candidates that were springing up out of the woodwork. Since Carter's organization was quite weak in California, I offered my services to his campaign manager, and was made coordinator for Riverside Country. I worked hard in the next six months, and although Carter lost the California primary to Brown by a wide margin, the congressional districts in my area went predominately for the Southerner, and my work came to the attention of the statewide coordinator. I was eventually made his second-in-command in August, 1976, and when Carter carried California in the November elections, I was offered my choice of two or three jobs in various federal agencies. On January 20, 1977, Jimmy became Lord President James VI Carter, and I joined the Department of Health, Education, and Welfare. I had already resigned my job in Riverside a year previously, and it was a simple matter to pull up my rather shallow California roots, and find a house in McLean, Virginia. Also about this time, I met my wife, and we were married shortly before I moved east.

MR. THOMAS: It must have been a very exciting period for you, sir.

THE PRESIDENT: And indeed it was, Mr. Thomas. Washington had become rather stale over the past eight years, and the election of a rural Southerner with no ties to the political establishment set the place on end. Carter certainly knew what he wanted, and he proposed a series of reforms that didn't rest too well with the establishment. In the end, he was forced to compromise on some parts of his plan, but he did manage to make the first significant improvements in the federal bureaucracy in several generations. My own career moved steadily forward, on several different fronts, since I was not only working for the government, but also pursuing my secret hobby of writing, under a pseudonym, of course.

MR. THOMAS: But I don't find any publications from that period listed in your vita, Lord President...

THE PRESIDENT: No, you wouldn't, Steve, since I kept these things absolutely hidden from my superiors, who would have frowned on such frivolities; and also for another reason; a writer tends to draw his characters and situations from the people and social groups he's had direct contact with and I found my working environment a gold mine for my fictions. And even though I disguised particular names, incidents, and personalities, the persons I worked with in those departments might have been able to pick themselves out had they known I was a writer. Some of my drawings-from-life were distinctly unflattering.

MR. THOMAS: Would you mind very much if I asked you what kinds of things you wrote?

THE PRESIDENT: I'd rather not be too specific, Steve, except to say that my particular forte was the short story, and I stayed primarily in the science fiction field. I've read and collected science fiction since the age of 9 or 10. In fact, Ms. Harrington, you may wish to note that I'm converting one of the upstairs bedrooms in the White House into my personal library, and may be forced to expand into a second room if I can't fit everything in. My collection numbers roughly 37,000 volumes, mostly paperbacks and other ephemera.

MR. THOMAS: If we could return to your career, Lord President.

THE PRESIDENT: Of course. I spent five years in Washington, rising eventually to an undersecretariat in the remains of HEW. Carter was reelected in 1980, beating out an obscure Michigan congressman named Leslie King, and I decided shortly thereafter to return to California, to seek my fortunes elsewhere. I practiced law for a year, and then ran for Congress from the 45th district in 1982.

MR. THOMAS: And you were elected.

THE PRESIDENT: So it seems. I'd maintained my contacts with local political leaders while I was in Washington, and it wasn't that difficult to increase them once I was back home. Getting the Democratic nomination was actually quite easy, since nobody wanted it; in those days, that part of California still tended to vote Republican. And I was up against an incumbent. But I ran a campaign based on her own record, and as the gods would have it, I won.

MR. THOMAS: And were reelected again in the '84 vote, I believe.

THE PRESIDENT: Yes. That was a strange year. Carter was leaving office, after eight successful (but tiring) years of officiating over a bureaucracy he was never quite able to break. The Democrats nominated a liberal senator, Donald Hansen, and the Republicans a conservative Nevada governor, Gerald Freedman. Then a group of dissatisfied Carterite Democrats broke away from the party, formed a new political organization they called the National Caucus, and nominated a Southern moderate, Jeb Stuart Green. The resulting split in the party's hierarchy gave the election to the Republican nominee, who carried most of the west and midwest, while Hansen took the northeast, and Green the south and one or two western states. The key states turned out to be California and Illinois, and they both went to Freedman by narrow margins. The House and Senate remained Democratic, as they'd been for almost thirty years. Freedman was sworn in early in 1985, and was immediately faced with his first crisis, as South Africa was finally invaded by its black neighbors. Rhodesia had fallen in 1980 to the combined forces of guerrilla uprisings, troop incursions from Mozambique, and the empty rhetoric of its own regime, but the Republic of South Africa was much more firmly entrenched, and had resisted all attempts at internal reform. Finally, the Black African League put together a fighting force financed by the Arabs, and invaded Namibia, the first of its objectives. Unfortunately, the expedition seemed doomed from the very beginning, as the desert and South Africa's superb army combined to destroy one fighting force, and severely cripple another. The BAL withdrew its men to the peripheries of Namibia, and began guerrilla fighting. Then both appealed to the US for assistance. I was a second-termer in the House at the time, and I can recall our astonished reactions when Freedman announced that the United States would send economic assistance and military advisers to the South African forces. I asked for the floor, and immediately began questioning the wisdom of sending more of our troops overseas; had not this policy already proved disastrous in the 1960s? But even as I was speaking, transport planes were speeding across the Atlantic towards the east, filled with American soldiers. I continued to speak out during the ensuing weeks, and even made a motion to cut off funds for the expedition; regretably, however, the budget had been passed several weeks earlier, and the military had more than enough leeway to work with. By Christmas we had 10,000 troops in Africa. Then the casualities started flowing back, and in April of 1986 I co-sponsored a resolution censuring the Lord President for acting without proper consultation with Congress. The public uproar finally reached the point where Freedman was forced to withdraw all American "advisers," and greatly reduce military aid. Meanwhile, a popular California senator had announced his retirement, and I was urged to run for the seat. I filed in March. I trounced my Democratic opponent in the June primary, and then found myself facing two serious contenders in the fall elections. Jeb Stuart Green had refused to bury himself in a political grave after his defeat in 1984, and instead had begun organizing his renamed National Party at the local level, beginning with the southern and southwestern states. He fielded candidates for offices in about twenty states in 1986, including California. And his people did surprisingly well, taking one governorship, two senate seats, eight seats in the House of Representatives, and many local offices. Although I won my race, the National Party candidate was a clear second, the Republican fading to third.

MR. THOMAS: So you had finally reached the national political scene, at the age of forty.

THE PRESIDENT: I was sworn in on January 3, 1987; I can remember the day as clearly as yesterday, cold, windy, with a light rain wetting everybody's hair. Someone had decided to hold the swearing-in ceremonies outside that year (it's never been done since); one of my colleagues caught a bad cold that developed into pneumonia: he died after serving just two weeks, three days. Freedman's administration was rapidly going from bad to worse, as the economy began sinking into a recession. The poor man tried very hard, but he just wasn't intelligent enough to cope with one crisis after another, and his particular term seemed to be filled with them. It must have been a living nightmare for him. To make things even worse, the Republicans had lost ground in Congress in the '86 elections, both to the Democrats and Nationals, and were now in danger of being eclipsed as the opposition party. In the midst of all this, in the summer of 1987, a terrorist group intent on freeing Palestine from the Arabs seized an atom bomb in Iran, and flew it to Italy, threatening to blow up Rome unless their demands were met. Something went wrong with the negotiations, or possibly the gunmen were unfamiliar with the arming device; the bomb exploded, killing a half million Italians, included most of the Italian government, and Pope Paschal III. Freedman was blamed by some commentators for his intransigence in the bargaining, and the opinion polls dropped to a 15% approval rating for his presidency. Rather wisely, I think, he chose not to run for reelection in 1988, and in his place the Republicans nominated Alex Foresman, Senior Senator from the state of Texas. I had sponsored a jobs bill early in 1988 that drew much favorable attention from commentators, and had generated some public response, and I was urged by many of the party regulars to run for the presidency. I reluctantly allowed my name to be used, and won several primaries in the spring, although I never actively campaigned. The leading candidate for the Democratic nomination was Jacob Silverberg, Governor of New York, although Albert Sanders, a senator from Illinois, also ran well in the early stages of the campaign. The convention was scheduled for July, and after the California primary, Silverberg had about 1300 votes, Sanders a thousand or so, and I had roughly 700. Since it was clear to me that I had a poor shot at the nomination, I talked with both candidates about the possibility of supporting one or the other, discussing their views and positions on many different subjects, and trying to see what kind of lord president either of them would make. I felt then, as I do now, that only a man with moderate views could be elected, and since Sanders was much more oriented towards the middle-of-the-road, I released my delegates, but urged them to support Sanders for the nomination. Al Sanders won on the second ballot, and when I called to give my congratulations, offered me the Vice-Presidency. I accepted.

MR. THOMAS: And you won a resounding victory at the polls.

THE PRESIDENT: Something like 55% of the vote, as I recall. Al and I took our oaths on January 19, 1989. Unfortunately, no one has ever managed to find very much for Vice Presidents to do, except wait around for the Lord President to die, and that's a rather morbid subject from any point of view. Al kept me briefed, and I was asked to represent the US on several different occasions overseas (I was in France, for example, for the state funeral of King Henri VI in 1990, and visited Don Pedro IV of Brazil in 1992), but other than that we kept a cordial distance, and I was left pretty much alone to do as I pleased. I did make a number of trips to local party headquarters and functions, and in this way I met a great many politicos that I would otherwise never have known. Al was having his problems with Congress, since the Nationals had increased their representation in the 1988 elections substantially, although their presidential nominee, Green, did worse the second time around. Still, between the declining reputations of the Republicans, and the ascending fortunes of the Nationals, they controlled a majority of the seats in the House, and almost a majority in the Senate, and they made the most of it. Al was forced to veto a number of bills sent across his desk, and had several of his most important proposals sent down to defeat. The situation got so bad that I was called over to his office one day, and asked to set up a liaison office between the White House and Congress. Since each party controlled one house, there was some basis for compromise on most issues, and I was able to mollify the opposition on several key bills, enough, at least, to get them passed. The National Party swept the congressional elections in '90, taking both houses outright, while Republican forces were virtually extinguished; rather ominously for the latter, several prominent Republican politicians switched their party registration to the Nationals shortly afterwards, starting a trend which has continued to this day. In the spring of 1991, I was working in my office when I received an urgent telephone call: Lord President Sanders had suffered a stroke, and was in critical condition at Bethesda Naval Hospital. The cabinet met immediately, and asked me to assume the temporary role of Acting Lord President, which I did. I requested TV time from the networks, and reported the situation to the American people, emphasizing that I would exercise the powers of Acting Lord President only until Sanders had regained his faculties.

MR. THOMAS: There were no written procedures covering an emergency of this type. Did everyone agree that you should take over?

THE PRESIDENT: For the most part, yes, although there were one or two members of the cabinet who felt that the entire issue should be postponed until the immediate crisis passed. I think they believed the situation might resolve itself if Sanders died.

MR. THOMAS: What were your own feelings on the subject?

THE PRESIDENT: I was very hesitant to assume the role required of me, for several reasons: on the one hand, there really isn't any such thing as an "Acting" Lord

President: you either are or your aren't, and unless Albert Sanders died, I wasn't. Hence, I could only expect limited support for anything that I might try to do. My primary purpose was to keep the seat warm until the legitimate occupant of the chair returned, and not to initiate any astounding new policies or legislation of my own. I would be expected to handle any emergencies that might arise, but that's about as far as I could go. And if in fact I had tried to do anything else, I'm quite sure that the cabinet and virtually every other government agency (and possibly Congress) would have objected. In other words, I had no legal status, I was serving specifically at the pleasure of the cabinet, and my role was strictly limited. But, as luck would have it, I *was* able to accomplish something in spite of them all.

MR. THOMAS: That was the famous Monaco Summit, wasn't it?

THE PRESIDENT: Yes, Steve. For some time. we'd been having difficulties with the Russians on the Moon, as each big power kept claiming encroachment into its respective base territories. Finally, it started to get nasty, when several pressure chambers were mysteriously punctured by pellets shot from air cannon. The Soviets had threatened a small war after one of their higher-ranking officers was killed, so I immediately proposed a meeting with People's Tsar Mikhail Antonovich Dzhuginin, on a neutral territory halfway between our countries. Dzhuginin agreed, and Prince Albert II of Monaco volunteered his services. They even cleared out one of the casinos for us. The result was the Treaty of Monte Carlo, which specified the rights, obligations, and limitations of each party in outer space, and established a series of guidelines to be used by national groups in colonizing other planetary bodies, whatever their size. The Senate promptly ratified the document, and several other countries have added their signatures in the intervening decade. More importantly, perhaps, the rules seem to work, and we've had few troubles in space with the Russians ever since. After three months as Acting Lord President, I was told that Al was well enough to resume his duties, and I reverted to my previous lazy existence.

MR. THOMAS: When did you decide to run for the lord presidency?

THE PRESIDENT: It was quite clear to me

that Sanders was unfit to run for a second term, and he confirmed that publicly in late 1991. After consulting with party officials, I announced my candidacy in December of that year. At about the same time, one of my oldest rivals, Jack Nelson, longtime Senator from Oregon, also announced. Jeb Stuart Green again indicated his willingness to try for the National Party ticket, but met with desultory response; more enthusiasm was shown for Richard Rogers, Governor of Florida. Only one man, former Vice President Conway, indicated much interest in the Republican label, and he was ultimately nominated in June. I'd been in politics long enough by this time to acquire both friends and enemies, and it turned out that I had more of the former, because I won the nomination on the first ballot in Los Angeles, soundly defeating Nelson by over 500 votes. The Nationals nominated Rogers by an overwhelming majority. The campaign was fought over several issues of immediate importance, including aid to famine victims in India and Bangladesh, inflation, and taxes, and I found myself forced to defend many things over which I'd had no control (typical of the lot was the slogan, "remember the one dollar stamp?"). I suddenly got behind in the polls, and I was never quite able to catch up, although the final margin on election day was only about 4%. Rogers was in, and I was on my way to a premature retirement.

MR. THOMAS: Had you made any plans prior to that time contingent upon losing?

THE PRESIDENT: Not really. I'd briefly considered the possibility, but I had too much else to do, and there never was really an opportunity to go over the alternatives. I thought about writing a few novels out of my system, but that particular time of my life had passed, and I soon became bored with my attempts. I also considered going back into law, but I'd been so long absent from the legal scene that I was unfamiliar with recent legal history, and didn't particularly feel inclined to catch up gain. So I tried doing a few analyses of modern political times, and enjoyed the research so much that I actually started piecing together a book on the subject; as you know, it sold very well indeed. This led to a second history, plus a series of commentaries in various semischolarly reviews. I also started work on the Kennedy book at about this time, although I didn't finish it until 1998. The Nationals took a drubbing in the elections of '94, and the Democrats regained control of Congress once again, for the first time in ten years. The Republicans by this point had shriveled to one or two senate seats, and 10-15 congressional districts, and were no longer a factor. I was urged privately to run again for the Democratic nomination in 1996, but declined for a variety of reasons, mostly personal. Del Sanders, Albert's brother, became the Democratic nominee, and Rogers, of course, was renominated by the Nationals. Rogers used his incumbency well, and the Demos were soundly defeated. The Nationals regained the House. During this period I stayed out of the bright lights of public life, preferring to enjoy the leisure time that I felt I'd earned; I did make a few public appearances, but kept them down to a minimum, primarily on the college circuit.

MR. THOMAS: What changed your mind about coming out of retirement?

THE PRESIDENT: Well, Steve, I got a little bored, and I very much missed being at the center of things. So I put out a few feelers to some of my old party friends around the fall of 1999, and they were well enough received that I tossed my name out in January of the following year. Del Sanders tried for the nomination a second time, but once again, I managed to come out on top. The National Party chose Alvero Douglas at its July convention. And as you're all aware, I won in the November elections by a large majority.

MR. THOMAS: In looking back over your career, do you have any regrets?

THE PRESIDENT: Well, I regret that I lost in 1992. *(laughter)* I suppose that everyone can remember times when he'd have done something differently. But hindsight is not a very useful tool when you're faced with an immediate problem, and you have to use the knowledge and wisdom that you have readily available to deal with it. If you've done your best, I can't see that you can be faulted for it. Yes, I have some regrets; but realistically, I try not to look backwards too often, lest I fall flat on my nose. Ms. Harrington.

MS. HARRINGTON: Lord President, I want to thank you for giving our audience such a detailed and interesting account of your career; I found it perfectly fascinating.

THE PRESIDENT: Thank you, Janet.

MS. HARRINGTON: Do you think the race
issue will cause you any problems?

THE PRESIDENT: No, I don't really think so.
We've become sophisticated enough in this country that
bigotry just isn't an issue any more. I can remember the
demonstrations and riots of the 1960s, and they seem to me
now to have occurred in some other lifetime. Attitudes have
changed, and while prejudice will exist as long as man exists, it
no longer seems to be a factor in American politics.

MR. PETERSON: What are your feelings on
the space race?

THE PRESIDENT: I think the next logical
step in the development of our resources in space is the
colonization of Mars. Our Moon bases have proved very successful in widening our perspectives in the natural sciences,
and I feel that Mars would prove even more valuable to the
human race in the long term. Such a program would, of course,
be enormously expensive, but the resulting technological
breakthroughs would more than pay for our investment, as
has been the case with every other space project we've under-
taken. I also think we should explore the possibility of sending
a probe to several nearby solar systems, realizing that they
would take centuries to reach their destinations, and designing
them accordingly. The challenge of putting together a mechanism that would literally survive the ages once again would have
numerous immediate benefits to earthly civilization. We've
pretty well surveyed our own solar system with various probes
and landers, and have come to the conclusion that ours is the
only planet with life. And only Mars and the Moon seem
worth colonizing at this point. The next logical step is sending
probes to the stars, and probing the stars for signals coming
back. I would support any programs aimed in this direction.

MS. HARRINGTON: Lord President, I wonder
if I could ask you a personal question?

THE PRESIDENT: Yes, of course, Janet.

MS. HARRINGTON: Do you sleep with your
wife, sir?

THE PRESIDENT: Well, I can't honestly see how that sort of thing could be of interest to anyone except my wife and myself, but if you really want to know the scandalous details, I have but one answer: yes.

MR. PETERSON: Have you chosen a motto for your administration?

THE PRESIDENT: "Efficiency is." Mr. Thomas.

MR. THOMAS: When will the presidential coin issue be ready?

THE PRESIDENT: I'm told by the Treasurer that the first coins, the five- and ten-dollar pieces, will be issued on February 1st, the others to follow as they're ready. I have a sample planchet stamped on the obverse with the new design, if you're interested. Ah yes, here it is. *(he hands it over)*

MR. THOMAS: I wonder if you could hold that up to our cameras, sir, like this. How's that, Jack? Just a little bit closer, Lord President. Yes, right there, please. This is the new obverse of the ten-dollar coin, showing the bust of Lord President Lister. The inscription reads, "James VII, Lord President of the United States." Thank you very much, sir.

MS. HARRINGTON: The stamp issue, I presume, will also be out shortly?

THE PRESIDENT: So I'm told. But I'm afraid I don't have any samples to show. Delivery is promised by March the First, according to the last word I had on the subject.

MR. PETERSON: Lord President Rogers is renowned for his patronage of the arts. What do you intend to do in this area?

THE PRESIDENT: I've long believed that the government should provide subsidies to artists, writers, and performers of all types, administered primarily on the local level, through state, county, or municipal agencies. The exact mechanism for distributing the funds could be worked out at some later date, but the basic principle of the thing should be established well in advance. There are a great many creative persons who've been forced into other professions because they couldn't make their talents pay. I regret this very much, because not only is the world deprived of their unique offerings, but all too often their creativity tends to dry up for lack of exercise. Government-distributed stipends would provide assistance where it's needed most. We should, however, be very careful to formulate administrative guidelines in such a way that bureaucratic control of the projects is kept to an absolute minimum. We're not looking for poet laureates to celebrate the birthdays of the state governors with epic poems, and any attempts to impinge upon the creative freedom of the persons involved should be immediately squelched. At the same time, I think we do have a right to expect some end result from each person's stipend; if we're going to be acting as *le grand patron*, we ought, I think, to get something in return for the American public to appreciate. The idea, after all, is to encourage creativity and creative works, and I don't think we want anyone to get the idea that this kind of program is a free ride on the treasury. Yes, Janet.

MS. HARRINGTON: I think our viewers might be interested in knowing what kind of cuisine will predominate at the White House during the next four years.

THE PRESIDENT: I enjoy all kinds of food — indeed, it's my one great vice — but I particularly enjoy Italian and Chinese cuisine (Manderin style), and, of course, American foods of all kinds. One of my favorite dishes is Peking duck served with green onions, which is really much more delectable than it sounds. I also enjoy Chinese soups, and soups of all kinds, although I've always felt the Chinese make the best soups in the world. Breads, pasta, rolls, all that fattening food — love it! I also like to have plenty of green vegetables and fruits on my table. (I was kidded all through childhood for my love of green beans), and I'm very definitely an ice cream freak.

MS. HARRINGTON: What's your favorite flavor, Lord President?

THE PRESIDENT: Pralines 'n' cream. Next question, Mr. Peterson. Or is it your turn, Mr. Thomas?

MR. THOMAS: Thank you, sir. I don't

believe we've said anything this evening about the criminal statistics recently released by the Federal Bureau of Investigation. The Lord Director stated in a press conference on December 16th of last year that the overall crime rate for the country had once again increased significantly, for the 35th straight year, with murders up 6%, rape 2%, burglaries 11%, to name but a few. Your campaign speeches have presented a hard line towards repeat offenders. What kind of proposals do you intend to make to Congress regarding new criminal legislation, and what kind of policy changes do you expect to implement at the Department of Justice?

THE PRESIDENT: This is a particularly difficult question, Steve, and I'm not sure I can really provide too many details at this point. I firmly believe that there are some criminals who will never be rehabilitated, no matter how long we try, and these kinds of persons should never be released to prey on the public again. If that means building more prisons, so be it. Plea bargaining should be eliminated at once, and more appropriate sentencing introduced, with a wider range of options available to each justice. Habitual criminals, those convicted of similar offenses more than two times, are obviously trying to make a career of crime, and should be discouraged from doing so with extremely stiff sentences, and no possibility of parole. A life sentence should mean just that. Organized crime can be fought in just one way, with large sums of money, and a police force specially organized to deal with the problem, and I propose we try both. Victimless crimes, such as the laws against marijuana that still remain on some states' books, should be reduced to misdemeanors, with appropriate sentencing. We ought to treat criminals the same way we treat all citizens, with fairness and justice, but we should not go out of our collective paths to grant any of them special rights or privileges.

MR. THOMAS: Do you favor capital punishment?

THE PRESIDENT: Well, sometimes I have, and sometimes I haven't. I don't mean to be a fence-straddler on this question, but it's very hard to say that capital punishment is right or wrong in all cases. I think there are perhaps some few instances where it seems the only appropriate answer to a particularly heinous crime; but even in those situations, it should be a remedy that's exceedingly difficult to apply, with the Lord President making the final determination. It's the possibility of error that frightens me; we're all fallible human beings, and we all have the potential of making mistakes, and to make a mistake with a man's life is something I'd hate to be sleeping with. I can recall several cases from the 1920s and '30s where an innocent or probably innocent man was executed for something he didn't do. Does that answer your question?

MR. THOMAS: Well, yes, I think so, except that I'd like to know what crimes you would consider appropriate for the death penalty.

THE PRESIDENT: Murders which involve deliberate mutilation, torture, or sex deviation; kidnapping with the murder of the victim-for-sale; terrorist crimes involving the death of one or more individuals, or the threat of mass murder (for example, the Rome affair); political assassinations of US officials or foreign dignitaries; hijackings that involve death or injury to innocent passengers; treason (the real thing, not the spy dramas of screen and stage).

MR. PETERSON: During Lord Rogers' administration, several laws were passed restricting press coverage of trials, at the discretion of the presiding judge or judges. How do you feel about this sort of action?

THE PRESIDENT: I oppose it, and will seek to have that particular law revoked. Throughout our legal history, we have always made an effort to have the public represented at every trial in which a man's fate is determined by a jury of his peers. The television camera or the reporter is, in my opinion, merely an extension of this right, and indeed, carries it to its logical conclusion. By restricting the public's right to see judicial proceedings, we are in effect saying that the average American citizen is incapable of making a fair decision based on the evidence at hand.

MR. PETERSON: But the judicial officers who advocate restricting media coverage say they must do so to protect the rights of the defendant. Too much coverage, so the argument goes, may so prejudice a particular case that a fair trial will be impossible to obtain in a particular geographical area.

THE PRESIDENT: I don't believe it for a

minute. Under such circumstances, I would go out of my way to be fair and open-minded to the accused, and I think that most Americans would follow suit. You know, Miles, I've been selected several times in my career to serve on juries, and I've always been impressed by the seriousness with which potential jurors take their duties. They were all very minor trials, of course, the kind that never reach the 6 o'clock news, but they were also the type where the police had an open-and-shut case. Most of these cases get guilty verdicts when they actually go to trial, because the marginal ones tend to get weeded out along the way; either the judge drops the whole thing for lack of evidence, or the attorney for the defendant makes him plead guilty to a lesser charge. Once in awhile the poor chump tries to tough it out, but they've usually got him dead-to-rights. Well, the cases on which I sat were all of this type; and yet, I remember very distinctly how meticulously we sifted through the evidence and testimony, looking for any shred of uncertainty in the prosecution's case. We didn't find any, and were forced to render a judgment of guilty, with a great deal of regret. Americans are not children, and we should give them credit for having the intelligence to take into consideration whatever special circumstances might pertain to a particular trial.

MS. HARRINGTON: Do you intend to appoint any women to the supreme court or your cabinet?

THE PRESIDENT: Well, I suppose so; do you intend to hire a male secretary to type your correspondence? I have several women under consideration for cabinet positions, but then again, I also have several men who might qualify, not to mention a couple of Australian sheep dogs. Ms. Harrington, I don't select persons for administrative posts because they have green hair and fleas; it's quite the other way around, let me assure you, and their physical or sexual attributes are purely incidental. I try to pick the best person for the job. As far as the Supreme Court is concerned, I'll deal with that question when there's a vacancy. Mr. Thomas.

MR. THOMAS: While we're on the subject of courts and the press, do you favor the bill currently before the Congress that would grant the press immunity from revealing confidential sources to a judge or jury?

THE PRESIDENT: I do in general, although I can envision several possible scenarios where such a privilege could and should be waived. Thus, I would prefer having some means of reviewing the situation by a higher court, which could then insist that the reporter's right of confidentiality be dropped if the circumstances warranted.

MR. THOMAS: Isn't this leaving a great deal of leeway to the judicial system?

THE PRESIDENT: Not really. I think the general principle should be confidentiality, with the provision that special cases could be appealed. We should attempt to make the appeal process as difficult as possible.

MR. THOMAS: What kind of circumstances, in your opinion, would justify a waiver?

THE PRESIDENT: A matter of life and death, certainly. You could say, of course, that any responsible newsman would gladly waive his rights himself in such an eventuality, and for the most part, I think you'd be perfectly right. But there are a few reporters who are not responsible, since irresponsible people seem to appear in every profession, and it is for these kinds of people that such laws are written, to protect the many and control the few.

MS. HARRINGTON: How do your children feel about your new home?

THE PRESIDENT: Adam is only here part of the time anyway, so I'm not really too sure what he thinks. He did say he likes the swimming pool. Jennie seems to spend most of her time plotting with her mother about all the redecorating they intend to do. And as far as old Blue's concerned, he doesn't really seem to mind what's going on as long as all of us are here.

MS. HARRINGTON: I believe he was a stray; is that correct?

THE PRESIDENT: Yes, Janet, he just wandered by one day. I started feeding him, and over a period of months he became one of the family.

MR. PETERSON: Sir, we're running out of

time, but before we leave, I wanted to ask you one more question.

THE PRESIDENT: Yes, Miles.

MR. PETERSON: Who's your favorite president, the one man among your predecessors whom you most admire?

THE PRESIDENT: Well, I'd have to say John Kennedy, I think, for many reasons. He wasn't our greatest lord president, by any measurable standard, and the man certainly had his faults — he was as human as the rest of us. But he was intelligent, capable, and exceptionally likeable, with a remarkable sense of humor. I had the opportunity of meeting him not long before he died, and I remember every minute of that conversation to this day. He was a spell-binder; when he talked, you listened. As I mentioned earlier in this interview, I was greatly shocked by that tragic November day in Dallas, when Kennedy was shot and Connally killed; in a real sense, my own destiny has been shaped by what I saw and heard that afternoon. Strangely enough, whenever I've talked about it with others of my generation, they all seem to remember just what they were doing that fall day, when the first announcement came over the radio. For all of us, I think, it was a sudden realization of man's mortality. Here was this dynamic, charismatic leader, with his young, beautiful wife, and several small children, suddenly wounded near to death, and everyone of us hanging over that thin thread, waiting morbidly to see if it finally parted or managed to hold on. We all wondered what would become of us if our leader died. And I myself have wondered ever since. It's the oldest question in history: do the times make the man, or the man the times? Did Napoleon suddenly surface because the times were ready for him, or did he make his own crawl to the top, thereby changing history forever? I don't know. I am convinced, though, that the world teetered that day on the brink of something, whether good or ill I'll never know, and that a gunman's slight waver when he pulled his trigger changed the course of history. And I wonder again sometimes — this is the science fictional part of me — whether there isn't a world somewhere where Kennedy was killed and Connally wounded, where a lord president named Lyndon Johnson served out Kennedy's term, where perhaps we never got involved in Vietnam. An idle speculation, I suppose, but one of vital interest to historians. I remember a curious incident that morning in Dallas, when Kennedy and his wife were just getting into their car; Kennedy got into the back seat for the first part of the trip, but after travelling a few blocks, he began complaining of pains in his back, and Connally offered to change seats. Kennedy turned him down, but Jackie Kennedy insisted that he move up front, and he finally took her advice. They briefly stopped the cavalcade, and the two men switched positions. A few miles later, three shots rang out amidst the cheers of a sparse crowd, and both men slumped over in their places. Two of the bullets had hit Connally, splitting his head apart, and piercing his neck and shoulder, and one had continued on through his body to hit Kennedy, wounding him in several places. The Texas governor died shortly after reaching the hospital; Kennedy remained in critical condition for a number of days. Lyndon Johnson was sworn in as Acting President on a plane at Dallas International Airport, and managed to keep things moving until Kennedy returned to the Executive Office in 1964.

MR. PETERSON: If Kennedy had been killed then, do you think history's verdict of his administration would be any different today?

THE PRESIDENT: Oh, I'm sure of it, Miles. Consider for a moment the case of Lord Lincoln, who was shot in the back of his head in April, 1865, just after the Civil War had been won. Honest Abe was adulated as no lord president ever had been, and that aura of reverence continues to this day: most historians regard him as one of this country's greatest leaders. But think for a moment: what would his reputation have been had his assassination occurred a year or two before or after it actually happened. A year earlier, Lincoln had been in serious political trouble; the Democrats, spurred on by the inconclusive nature of the war, looked like sure winners in the fall elections. And there wasn't much reverence being shown the president then: politicians, commentators, and even ordinary folk lampooned the Illinois bumpkin for his ungangly ways, homely face, and country-style humor. A lot of people resented Abe's success, a great many more resented his backwoods origins, and a number of others were just plain jealous. There's another alternative; let's say that Lincoln's guard at the Ford Theater had done his job properly, and John Wilkes Booth had been intercepted and arrested as he tried to enter the gallery behind the Lord President's box.

Abe had nearly four more years to go in his term. The Radical Republicans controlled Congress, and were utterly determined to make the south pay a price for its audacious revolution. And, of course, in real history they had their way, completely overwhelming the hapless administration of Andrew Johnson, and nearly succeeding in disposing of him as well. Would Lincoln have fared any better? Some historians don't think so; others say that he would most certainly have been more adroit at dealing with Congress, but still would have faced one confrontation and crisis after another. Remember, Andrew Johnson was only trying to carry out Lincoln's program for reconciliation with the south. Almost all of his proposals were actually borrowed from Abe's top hat. So you see, in both cases, Lincoln's reputation could have come down to us in completely different form, had he only died a little sooner or a little later. Kennedy's case is very similar. If Kennedy had actually been killed at Dallas, I'm quite certain he would have been revered by everyone far beyond his actual humanity. His defects and weaknesses would have been largely forgotten, and his handsomeness, good humor, and decisiveness would have expanded to fill the gap. He would have been touted as the most beloved American lord president of the twentieth century.

MR. PETERSON: But of course, it didn't happen that way.

THE PRESIDENT: No, Miles, it didn't, and in a way I'm sorry it didn't; the man perhaps deserved better than he got. After he returned to Washington, Kennedy found things subtly changed. On the one hand, he encountered that certain amount of sympathy that one always receives with any serious illness or disability, and I think he found this difficult to cope with; after all, he'd always been a very athletic man, and he wasn't used to thinking of himself in quite those terms. And on the other side, Lyndon Johnson had managed in the interim to get a large amount of legislation passed that Kennedy had been pushing for years with little success, and I think that he felt that Johnson had gone behind his back to do it. Lyndon thought he was just doing his job, and he saw no particular reason why he shouldn't use his old legislative contacts to get a few things done. So they had an immediate falling-out, and the result was Senator Humphrey's nomination for Vice-President in the '64 convention. Kennedy rode his convalescent popularity into a second term, but it wasn't long before weeds began growing in Camelot. The legislative successes that Johnson had managed to engineer in early 1964 faded away, and the Vietnam War began growing bigger and bigger. All of Kennedy's advisers, both military and civilian, felt that the United States needed to support Vietnam, or lose all of southern Asia. So the war began escalating, we sent them troops, the troop levels went higher and higher, and soon we had hundreds of thousands of men in another country, fighting a war that wasn't really ours, with a steadily-increasing casualty list. Ironically, the 1964 campaign against Goldwater had been based almost entirely on war fears, highlighted by the infamous commercial showing an atomic bomb exploding, the implication being that Goldwater's election would lead immediately to war.

MR. PETERSON: Do you think Kennedy could have found a way out of the Vietnam crisis once we had committed ourselves?

THE PRESIDENT: Not very easily. The entire military establishment supported the war, as did most of the civilian men in Kennedy's government. I think they all felt that the Cuban crisis had come about because America hadn't shown enough willingness to slug it out with the Russians everywhere they had given us a shove, and that we now had an opportunity to spit back in their collectivated faces. The real truth of the matter was never perceived: we were getting ourselves involved in a civil war that would never end until we withdrew, and despite our material advantages, in the long run we'd lose unless we were willing to kill off everyone living in the north. The French had learned that in 1954, and fools that we were, we were repeating history.

MR. PETERSON: But wasn't Kennedy responsible for American involvement? How then can you call him a great lord president?

THE PRESIDENT: Yes and no; the actual American involvement started with Eisenhower. However, Kennedy did escalate our military presence considerably, and he must, of course, take the ultimate responsibility for sending American troops overseas. I don't call him the greatest lord president of our times, but I do feel that he was very much a tragic figure, who was badly advised and badly served by those under him. That doesn't excuse his actions, but it does place them into perspective. Kennedy's popularity declined with the increased American presence in southeast Asia, and by the time he left office in 1969, he was at his lowest point ever, a 25% approval rating. He retired to his estate in Massachusetts, and lived a limbo existence for the next twenty years, dying in 1989. History had overtaken him, and left him limp and worn out before his time, and the few pictures we have of him from those later years show a thin, haggard man with hollow eyes, the portrait of a man haunted by his own past. If one could only change history . . .

MR. PETERSON: Lord President, I want to thank you for agreeing to appear on the Public Eye on the eve of your inauguration. I know you must be a very busy man, and we all appreciate you taking time out from a busy schedule to talk with us.

THE PRESIDENT: Thank you, Miles; it's been my pleasure, believe me.

MR. PETERSON: This is Miles Peterson, representing the Independent Broadcasting System, and my colleagues are Steven Thomas of the FCN, and Janet Harrington from the *Washington Digest*. Our guest tonight has been the Hon. James Lister, who will be sworn in tomorrow as James VII, 42nd Lord President of the United States. Be sure to tune in again at this same time next week, when Don Augustin IV, Emperor of Mexico, will come under the scrutiny of the Public Eye. Thank you all, and good night.

www.ingramcontent.com/pod-product-compliance
Lightning Source LLC
Chambersburg PA
CBHW050915120626
46552CB00004B/1589